ANOTHER CELEBRATED DANCING BEAR

Gladys Scheffrin-Falk

Etchings by Barbara Garrison

CHARLES SCRIBNER'S SONS · NEW YORK

Collier Macmillan Canada • Toronto
Maxwell Macmillan International Publishing Group
New York • Oxford • Singapore • Sydney

A NOTE ABOUT THE PICTURES

In etching, a metal plate is covered with a resinous ground resistant to acid. The artist draws through the ground with a needle. The artist may also paint the ground in certain areas. The plate is then immersed in an acid solution that eats away the exposed metal. This may be repeated many times. To print, the etcher cleans the ground, forces ink into the etched areas, wipes off surface ink, and places the plate on the press, face up and covered with a damp 100 percent-rag paper. Felt blankets are placed on top and the plate is run through the press. Barbara Garrison prints with burnt-umber ink and then applies watercolor washes to each individual print.

Charles Scribner's Sons Books for Young Readers
Macmillan Publishing Company · 866 Third Avenue, New York, New York 10022
Collier Macmillan Canada, Inc.
1200 Eglinton Avenue East, Suite 200 · Don Mills, Ontario M3C 3N1

Printed in the United States of America
First Edition   10 9 8 7 6 5 4 3 2 1

Library of Congress Cataloging-in-Publication Data
Scheffrin-Falk, Gladys.
Another celebrated dancing bear / Gladys Scheffrin-Falk.
—1st ed.   p.   cm.   Illustrations by Barbara Garrison.
Summary: Boris receives dancing lessons from his friend Max,
a dancing bear with the Moscow Circus.
[1. Bears—Fiction. 2. Dancing—Fiction. 3. Friendship—Fiction.]
I. Garrison, Barbara, ill.   II. Title.
PZ7.S1942An 1991   [E]—dc20   89-13152 CIP AC
ISBN 0-684-19164-4

ANOTHER CELEBRATED
DANCING BEAR

To "Mr. Sabath," who was my violin teacher,
and to all the patient, devoted teachers like him
who show children how to make music and sing and dance

G.S.-F.

For Sparky

B.G.

In the days of the Czar there lived two bears who were excellent friends. Boris was a heavy-footed brown bear whose heart was soft as butter.

Max—short for Maximovich—was taller than Boris and always seemed quite elegant. That is, he was elegant for a brown bear. The fact is that Max was a dancer.

Yes, a dancer in the Moscow Circus.

One evening Boris stopped by his friend's apartment after work. He was feeling glum, as bears sometimes do. Max greeted him with a wave.

"Come in, Boris. Let's have some tea, shall we?"

"Oh, that would be something," Boris said. Max helped him off with his heavy work jacket and hung it in the hall closet.

Then Max put the samovar to boil.

On the wall in the dining room Boris saw a magnificent poster in gay colors and fancy letters.

"Coming to St. Petersburg next week! Max, THE CELEBRATED DANCING BEAR!" Boris read.

Max placed the samovar on the table. He set out two glasses and two plates. He sliced a lovely, fresh Russian bread that was a warm brown color, almost the same color as Max himself.

Before Boris knew it, two large tears rolled down his fuzzy brown cheeks.

"Boris, what is it?"

"What a fine poster! Traveling to St. Petersburg? How…how wonderful."

Max poured the tea.

"Some preserves, Boris?"

Boris nodded. He spread strawberry preserves on a thick slice of bread. He took a gulp of steaming tea.

"Boris, you rascal." Max raised his glass. "I believe you are jealous."

"Jealous? But who wouldn't be? You travel, the band plays, you dance before a cheering audience. Ahhh…"

"But, Boris, I know many who envy you because you work at the animal hospital. They think it must be marvelous to help animals who have been injured or have sore throats."

"Envy me? All I do is walk around with a pencil behind my ear. I see to it that the elephants and the monkeys and tigers take their medicine. When the lions roar and the tigers snarl, I make a list of the foods they don't like."

Max rose to his full height. "Why can't you also dance?"

"Yesterday, Max, my pencil slid off my ear and down inside my jacket collar. Of course, I couldn't reach it. Do you know what those monkeys did?"

"If you want to dance, I will teach you," Max said.

"They thought it was the funniest thing they had ever seen. Pointing at me, giggling and laughing. Oh, if I had had a bucket of water—"

"Of course I will teach you." Max waved his spoon at Boris. "When I come back from St. Petersburg. Your first lesson will be Monday after dinner. Lessons will be Mondays, Wednesdays, and Fridays. Seven o'clock to eight. What do you say to that, Boris, old friend?"

Boris swallowed the last of his bread and preserves. He sipped the last of his tea.

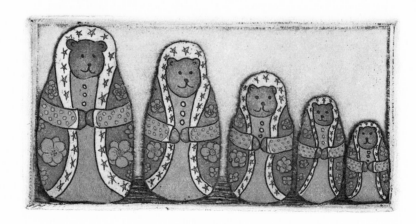

"You really think I could learn?" he asked.

"I am going to teach you," Max said.

At the door the friends embraced. Boris was trembling.

"I won't sleep," he said. He beamed at Max. "I'm so excited."

Max stood in the doorway and waved to Boris.

Boris hurried back to his friend. He thanked Max again for the tea—for the offer of dancing lessons—for everything!

Max laughed and waved good-night again.

Would he be able to learn, Boris wondered, as he strolled along Petya Street. He felt a little foolish. Dancing lessons at his age!

But the moon shone overhead on Petya Street. She seemed to say, "How wonderful to dance!"

So slowly the week passed. Max was away in St. Petersburg.

At the hospital, Boris was kept busy. Some of the big cats were being shifted about. Oh, Leo the lion would have plenty to roar about now!

When Boris drew near the monkeys, they crowded into a
pyramid. Some of them still had casts on legs and paws, but there
was no keeping them in bed. Now they pointed casts and paws at
Boris, all giggling and chattering away.

"Having fun?" Boris asked them, chewing on his pencil.

Finally…Monday. Boris was at Max's door on the dot of
seven.

"Am I too early?"

"You are on time," Max said. "Tonight we learn one step. One simple step. With this step, Boris, you will be able to dance a thousand evenings and a thousand different dances. And no one will realize that you know but one step."

The lesson began. One—two—three—four. One—two—three —four. Boris had to walk in rhythm, then glide. He glided forward and backward. He glided first to one side, then to the other.

Max put a record on the phonograph. Soon Boris was gliding to the music.

"Good," said Max. "You see how easy it is?"

"Am I dancing? Am I really dancing?" cried Boris.

"My dear friend, you are really dancing. Now we rest."

Boris was pleased to see that Max had put the samovar to boil.

Boris went home gliding on his toes all the way. Heads swiveled up and down Petya Street. He knew he must look strange—even comical.

But he was too excited to stop gliding. Besides, he was afraid he would forget what he had learned.

"Ah, the joy of dancing," he murmured to the moon.

The moon smiled down at Boris. She seemed to move in time with Boris's gliding steps.

The weeks zoomed by. So much to learn. Sometimes Max frowned. Sometimes he told Boris to lift a foot higher or faster.

Sometimes Boris forgot which foot was his left, which was the right. "What a dumb bear I am," he mumbled.

But Boris knew that Max was a fine teacher. He knew that he must listen to everything Max said.

At home Boris practiced. He bought records and played them as he danced. When he was too tired to practice, he read books about famous dancers.

One evening, as the two bears were sipping tea, Max said, "Boris, I was thinking. I would like to try a new dance, the Dance of the Hussars. It is not easy. But I think you can do it. Shall we try?"

No doubt about it, this was a far cry from Boris's first lesson. This was tricky. There was kicking and leaping. There were fast, tricky little steps.

He had to keep careful time to the music. Boris kept step with Max the best he could. When the dance was over, he mopped his bear brow with a bright red kerchief.

"Would you like to come with me to Minsk, dear friend? Would you like to dance with me in the circus?"

Boris was not sure that he understood.

"Me?" he asked.

Max embraced his friend. "It would be a joy to dance together, wouldn't it?"

Tears sprang to Boris's eyes. "To think I was so foolish as to be jealous!"

"To think that I never gave you lessons before!"

Just for fun the two old friends struck up the Hussars' Dance. They grinned at each other, bowed, and applauded each other like two young cubs.

The samovar bubbled away. It, too, seemed pleased that now there would be two celebrated dancing bears!